Creative Writing Competition Winners 2012-2014

I0626316

Writers' Guild of Acadiana

An Anthology from the Writers' Guild of Acadiana

Lafayette, Louisiana

For information contact Neal Bertrand, publisher, at neal@CypressCovePublishing.com

ISBN: 978-1-936707-04-1 for paperback
ISBN: 978-1-936707-05-8 for mobi Kindle ebook
ISBN: 978-1-936707-06-5 for epub ebook

Library of Congress Control Number: 2015948652

Cypress Cove Publishing
P.O. Box 91195
Lafayette, LA 70509-1195
USA

Phone (888) 606-3257

EDITORS Neal Bertrand and John François
BOOK DESIGN AND PRODUCTION Jeremy Bertrand

Other Titles Published by Cypress Cove Publishing

- Down-Home Cajun Cooking Favorites
- Rice Cooker Meals: Fast Home Cooking for Busy People
- Slow Cooker Meals: Easy Home Cooking for Busy People
- Cajun Country Fun Coloring and Activity Book
- From Cradle to Grave: Journey of the Louisiana Orphan Train Riders
- Dad's War Photos: Adventures in the South Pacific
- A House for Eliza: The Real Story of the Cajuns
- Never Say Goodbye: Real Stories of the Cajuns

Visit CypressCovePublishing.com for our latest books.

Contents

What is the Writers' Guild of Acadiana?

The Writers' Guild of Acadiana (WGA) is an organization made up of local writers, published and unpublished, who meet the last Tuesday of each month to share and gain knowledge in the craft of writing. The organization's goals are to provide a strong support system for our members, one that includes networking opportunities, as well as workshops and motivational speakers.

We meet the last Tuesday of each month at 7 p.m. in Barnes & Noble in the back portion of the store. Come check us out. The first two visits are free. Our membership fee is $30.00 a year. Thereafter member fees are $25.00 a year. A family membership is $15.00 per member. Membership fees are due on January 1 of each year. When you become a member you will receive "La Plume," our monthly newsletter.

Our agenda usually features a guest speaker one month and a member reading program the next month. Each reader is given a five minute time limit. We start at 7 p.m. and usually end around 8:30 p.m. Barnes & Noble closes at 10, so there is extra time for mingling after the meeting is over.

Find a seat, relax and get ready for an interesting and motivational night. Our monthly speakers come in a variety of categories; published authors, illustrators, poets, historians, children's authors, motivational speakers, travel writers, bloggers, writers of memoirs, and more.

We are looking forward to meeting you! Please bring a friend and help us spread the news. WGA will encourage you to develop your creative imagination.

Barnes & Noble is located at:
5705 Johnston Street
Lafayette, LA 70503

Become a member of the Writers' Guild of Acadiana TODAY!
Here's how...
Mail us your complete contact information (name, mailing
address, phone numbers, email address) with membership fee.
New member fee is $30.00 and you receive a Book Bag! The
renewal fee is $25.00. Your fees must be received by mail
before your membership will become official.

Please mail your check or money order to:
Writers' Guild of Acadiana
P.O. Box 51532
Lafayette, LA 70505

Email questions to: info@WritersGuildAcadiana.org
Website: WritersGuildAcadiana.org

WGA current officers:

President: Sudie Landry
Vice President: Neal Bertrand
Secretary: Ashley Burleigh
Treasurer: Louis K. Broussard
Historian: Jeanette Poole
Publicist: Susie Perry
Newsletter Editor: Melissa Abraham
Contest Director: Sudie Landry
President Emeritus: Ro Foley
Web Mistress: Julia K. Broussard

INTRODUCTION

The Writers' Guild of Acadiana holds a regular writing contest for members called a "Prompt Competition." A prompt is a starter sentence assigned to create your story. Some would call it a hook. Each person creates their own story around that sentence. It is amazing to see the many creative stories that were written.
Here are the winning entries.
For information regarding our WGA, check out WritersGuildAcadiana.org.

Date: 11/20/14
Category: Poetry
Author: Louis K. Broussard Sr.
The Prompt: Time Is Never Lost

IS...lasts only a moment then casts away its identity.
WAS...is a past tense that is to be lost into eternity.
WILL BE...is like the rising sun, inside the moments
not yet begun.
What footprints on the sands of time
Which others see and then say, "Whose prints were
left behind?"
And then old earth lends its sigh,
"Another has passed into goodbye
Then leaving prints sometimes large and sometimes
small
A metaphoric chalice filled with nectar or with gall."
All the while, WAS...Awaits the world and awaits us
all
IS...lasts only a moment then recedes into the past
The only remains are the footprints cast.
Is time ever lost or just misplaced
With due diligence I have searched to find its trace
In an old amber bottle on some dusty shelf
Seen by a wandering man in search of himself
Between frayed pages of some old tattered book
Left in a dark corner begging for another look
Pressed into the oily hand stains upon an old shop
door
Like a piece of driftwood that lays upon a shore

It may be on a dusty trunk or in an old leather shoe.
Maybe it has been stilled in an old photograph or two.
Is it nailed to the side of that weathered old barn
Or is it on the rusty tractor on grandpa's deserted farm
The truth is that our time is never lost, only misused,
Misplaced, misunderstood, misdirected, or abused
Time is in each moment and moments cannot last
Time leaves a footprint never lost but always cast.

Date: Oct. 28, 2014
Category: Fiction
Author: Greg Foshee
The Prompt: This was the second time I saw him killed...
Title: Art Mimics Life

Growing up, I was blessed to have a crazy uncle that enjoyed challenging my senses. Although I later learned that he was a college professor who taught both the history of European art and philosophy, he was my favorite relative because he never hesitated to take me to museums and periodic art exhibitions. For whatever reason, he always wanted to get my opinion of art. In retrospect, I think he genuinely appreciated my complete honesty and sometimes brutal critique of art as seen through the eyes of a child. Regardless of his motive, I genuinely appreciated the fact that he seemed so interested in my opinions when the rest of the world around me didn't seem to care what I thought.

One day on the way home from an early American Indian Art exhibit, we were driving to my parent's house when suddenly my uncle's car swerved vehemently and he swore a loud curse word that I had never heard him utter before. My world turned black shortly thereafter as the car we were driving in careened into a ditch at an accelerated speed and I lost consciousness. I awoke on a metal and nylon stretcher and I saw my uncle on another metal stretcher being hoisted onto an ambulance with its lights brightly circulating around my being. My uncle lay completely still and one of the emergency workers at the time asked that I turn my head away from my uncle. It was apparent, even to a seven-year-old that he had died in the accident.

The following morning as I lay in my hospital bed, I was relieved to learn that my uncle was revived in the ambulance and that he had in fact survived the accident. Things changed afterwards and my mother never allowed me to spend quality time with my uncle again even though I had protested her ultimatum many times. Time passed and I was now a junior in college when my mother abruptly called to inform me of my uncle's sudden death from a massive heart attack.

Without hesitation, I temporarily dropped out of school and drove to his funeral home the following day. As I looked at him in the casket, I realized that this was the second time that I had seen him killed. I wanted to make certain that he was really dead this time as I reached down and squeezed his hand.

As I stood there looking down on his rigid body with my hand still clutching his, I suddenly recalled a lesson that he had taught me over a decade ago. He had explained art that mimicked life and that it was a constant state of evolution. The definition of beauty changes from generation to generation although the intrinsic nature of art remains constant throughout time. Suddenly it made me realize that life and death were married to one another and that it would soon be my time to impose my ideals on the canvas of life after my graduation. I could only hope I could craft such a meaningful impression on the world as he had in the years previous to mine.

Date: Sept. 30, 2014
Category: Memoirs
Author: Greg Foshee
The Prompt: I Remember When...

    I remember when I was a young child still viewing the world with innocent, unbiased eyes. The days on my grandfather's farm were sometimes long and at other times, short. Sometimes he made me work hard under a hot summer's day when fluffy white clouds slowly drifted by as I sweated tilling the soil. My grandfather was the first man to show me that life was not always full of fun and games. Just as importantly, he taught me the meaning of pride for a job well done when he directed the occasional compliment my way. Back in those days, a smile and a pat on the back from him made me feel more valuable than any paycheck I'd ever receive in adulthood.

    At night, I also remember falling asleep listening to thousands of singular raindrops bounce lightly off a thin corrugated metal roof during a slow moving shower. My grandmother would later tell me she would sometimes untie my shoes and place them under my bed because I would sometimes fall asleep while she was drawing water for my bath.

    I now think of my three children and I wish they too, could have such childhood memories.

But as my generation is gradually replaced by another, I fervently hope that they retain similar memories in the midst of learning life's hard lessons.

Date: Aug. 26, 2014
Category: Fiction Poetry
Author: L.J. Lowery
The Prompt: There is a guy sitting on a park
bench reading a newspaper...
Title: Guy on a Bench

There is a guy sitting on a park bench reading a
newspaper.
The headline reads "Violence in the Middle East".
We've all heard of the things going on there
The man thinks to himself "What an outrage".
As he flips straight to the sports page,
The headline reads "Dodgers on a Hot Streak".
Next comes a loud bang and a hole through the
paper.
You see, my hometown isn't much safer.
Where I'm from it's common to hear about
somebody catching a stray bullet.
Man, I wish these youngsters would cool it.
The same violence that's out there is in our land,
So why must the fate of a man or woman be left
in a random hand?
I'm sick of the violence.
The only thing worse is silence,
So I'm gonna teach,
I'm gonna preach
In pursuit of peace
Through poetry
Because disgust is all this world has shown me.

Date: July 29, 2014
Category: Fiction
Author: Nell Bolden
The Prompt: If a man is given the ability to go
back in time and change one event...
Title: Cardinal's Lullaby

In Louisiana, a newlywed couple starts their
lives in a beautiful two story home. Their
excitement builds as they fill it with antiques that
their grandparents had gifted them. In the
doorway, Jeremy and Angelique stand in awe
admiring their child's nursery. Jeremy wraps his
arms around her growing waist. She turns to him,
gently kisses his cheek and softly whispers in his
ear, "In two more weeks our Angel will be
sleeping and dreaming in the same bed as you
did."

At that moment the sun's rays reflect on
Angelique's flawless alabaster face and long
golden hair. Smiling, Jeremy realizes that he will
soon be holding their daughter in his arms, where
he can keep her safe and warm.

They paint the walls pastel lavender and the
trim accented with an icy white gloss. The sun
peeks through the white eyelet curtains, casting
soft grey shadows, dancing on the baby's bed that
Jeremy's father had built twenty-three years ago
when Jeremy was born.

The focal point of the nursery is the mahogany
baby bed that has intricate details of a cardinal's
magnificent wingspan on the head and foot of the

bed. Jeremy's father had hand carved music notes on the rails from the song Cardinal's Lullaby, by Ruth Elaine. Jeremy and Angelique loved it so much; together they made a unique mobile with its sweet song that completed the nursery.

Angel is born the first day of May. Her hair is dark like her father's and her skin alabaster, flawless like her mother's. Angel's dark emerald green eyes twinkle like sparkling stars, so full of life. Jeremy and Angelique feel a completeness they had never thought possible.

When Angel turns five, Jeremy and Angelique decide to take Angel to the Space and Rocket Center in Huntsville, Alabama. They read her bedtime stories about space travel, the universe, and the weightlessness in space.

Angel puts her Raggedy Ann doll, her crayons, a coloring book of rockets, and two disposable cameras that her daddy had bought her into her lavender suitcase that has her name on it in bright yellow, her favorite color.

In July, they are on their way to an exciting vacation. By sunset, they stop for dinner at the Loveless Cafe on the Natchez Trace. After dinner, they return to the scenic route. Angel colors yellow stars, blue rockets and red planets in her coloring book. When she gets tired and sleepy, she asks, "How much longer is it to Alabama?" He tells her that they are only halfway there.

Night falls and Jeremy glances at Angelique. She has dozed off. Looking in his rear view mirror, he sees that Angel has fallen asleep, too. She is still holding a red crayon in one hand and her coloring book lies open on her lap. He reaches over to get his size 3X t-shirt off the back of his seat to cover Angel.

The SUV swerves off of the road and begins flipping. Headlights light up treetops and limbs snap in two. Angelique wakes up to glass shattering and flying in all directions. The vehicle is in mid-air one moment, and then it suddenly crashes to the ground. Angelique is thrown forward with extreme force into the dashboard, hitting her head. Angel's car seat unfastens and she is knocked around against the frame of the SUV crushing her now motionless body.

Jeremy wakes up groggy, confused and panic-stricken in the hospital. He remembers what has happened to his family. He pulls out his IV and frantically runs up and down the halls calling out for Angelique and Angel. Hospital staff forcibly take him back to his room and heavily sedate him. Jeremy is in and out of consciousness for three days.

His doctor gives him the grim news. Angelique is suffering from amnesia, his precious Angel is on life support and it will be his decision whether to keep it on. Jeremy wheels himself into Angelique's hospital room. No matter what he says to her, she only pushes him away. She doesn't remember who he is, who Angel is or even who she is anymore.

When he sees Angel on life support, he is horrified. Her eyes are closed. He cannot see the star twinkles or the shine that filled her with life. Jeremy's only two reasons for living are taken away by the accident on the Natchez Trace.

Three years pass. Angelique still doesn't recognize Jeremy as her husband, nor does she acknowledge that she had a child whose life was cut short. Jeremy visits her often and she accepts his friendship. He has given her Angel's Raggedy Ann in hopes that she would remember and recover.

He has lunch once a week in downtown Lafayette. One day a stranger asked him a question. "If a man is given the ability to go back in time and change one event in his life, what would he change? If that man were you, what would you change?" His response is, "I would not have reached for my blue t-shirt to cover my daughter. Instead, I would have been content to watch an angel sleep."

That evening he visits Angelique and brings her a gift wrapped in lavender paper with a bright yellow ribbon around the box. Angelique opens the box and holds the mobile that they had made together for Angel. She turns the key and hears the song, Cardinal's Lullaby, and tears fall from her eyes. She reaches for Jeremy, gently kisses his cheek and softly whispers in his ear, "Take me home."

Date: June 24, 2014
Category: Nonfiction Memoirs
Author: Louis Broussard
The Prompt: Portrait of a Mother

I pass by the portrait of a mother every day that I am home. On my desk in my bedroom are the framed pictures of my mother and father. It has been thirty-seven years since Mom passed on to the Promised Land. The end wasn't welcome and the death was not peaceful for lingering with cancer throughout her body was devastating to her and all who attended to her needs.

At the time of mother's sickness I was living in Brandon, Mississippi and worked as a paper salesman. I got a company transfer to Lafayette so I could be near my mother and dad. I moved to Milton into the homestead of my dad's parents. It was an old home on the Vermilion River. I worked out of Lafayette for the company and saw mother frequently. She took chemo and radiation and it soon zapped her energy and quality of life. The cancer spread rapidly throughout her body as the chemo and radiation didn't stave off the cancer for long. When it was found on her lung, she entered the hospital.

I was in Mississippi when I got the devastating news from my sister. The phone rang and my sister began speaking. "Hey, Kendall. I'm calling with some bad news."

"Oh my goodness," I said, "is it curable? Will radiation and chemo help?" I asked.

"They can only try but this kind does not respond well," she said.

I began to cry almost uncontrollably which immediately caused my sister to do the same. My wife, my darling Julia, rubbed my back and shoulders in a compassionate loving way. This helped me to compose myself and to finish the conversation. I knew that my life was about to be altered in ways I could not imagine.

I reflected over the next few months of mother's life and of all the things she had done for me and Edith. Mother was orphaned as a baby when her mother died within a month after giving birth. Her mother had been living with her mother and dad. Mother was then raised by her grandmother and grandfather and her dad soon left the family to start over with a job at the sulfur mine in Sulphur, Louisiana. When mother reached middle school she moved in with her two first cousins, children of her mother's sister. She became as a sister to the two girls and the relationship remained this way until their deaths. Mother struggled with asthma which was at times, very serious. My father took her to various doctors and specialists trying to relieve her symptoms. Dad worked away for three weeks at a time and was home only one week. He was a tugboat captain and mother had to be both mom and dad to my sister and me. Too many nights I could hear my mother struggling with the wheezing and the sound of the atomizer being used. The squeeze of the bulb and the inhaling wheeze as she sucked the mist into her lungs. Mother had bags under her eyes from lack of sleep but she woke us on those school mornings, fixed us breakfast, and sent us off to school. When we returned from school, a hot supper was always cooked for us.

In the times of my marriage and before mother's illness, we made many visits to see her and dad. My mother always prepared meals and desserts that she knew were a favorite of mine. Her home is a place that my heart will always live, though a GPS cannot find it. It is a sanctuary with memories, a place of saneness, and a respite for emotions.

Her image is on my desk printed on Kodak paper behind a clear glass. Although it is no more alive than a shadow or a reflection, it helps to remind me that she is the source of my life and the many places within where she abides.

Date: May 27, 2014
Category: Nonfiction Poetry
Author: Carl Anderson
The Prompt: Ode to Mama

Distilled divinity encased in earthen
Estuaries of love fishing freely in
Ivory arcs and spirity spheres
Conveying emotions and care
Continuing devotion with fear
With cold shoulders or warm hugs
Stern words, backhand like clubs
And sometimes, eye rolls and shrugs
"Just because I say so, now enough."
But was it ever enough?
In youth, too much
Coming of age, ewe, yuck,
"Not in front of my friends, Ma."
But in truth, awe struck
And no matter how heavy the bags
Under the eyes, she'd still carry me
No matter how deep a sigh with
Disbelief in her eyes at my actions,
"It's ok, son," For only one tenth of
the one hundredth of a second distracted
From her love
Because a limitless form,
My favorite of youth, in her eyes
Forever her little boy
And for me, Forever Ma.

Date: Apr. 29, 2014
Category: Fiction
Author: Ashley Burleigh
The Prompt: The True Modern American Fantasy

"Modern American Fantasy," that was the genre I had assigned for my Creative Writing class. Jonathon was the last student to be reading. I had been so excited to see what type of fantasies my students would concoct. My mind brainstormed to new worlds, mystical creatures, and magic. Instead, my students seemed to have missed that the class was "creative" writing and had given me countless retellings of Twilight and The Walking Dead. One student even managed to combine Twilight with The Walking Dead. While sparkling zombies are unusual, they do not make for a very good story.

Jonathon stood in front of the class with his hands nervously gripping the podium. Then his legs began to shake and I wondered if the poor boy would even be able to read his story.

"This is a true story," he said.

"Mister Ryder, you are aware that the topic is Modern American Fantasy?" I interrupted.

"Yes, Ma'am, but what is Modern American Fantasy really? I mean zombies, werewolves, vampires; all these creatures are deeply embedded in our society. They seem more real to me than other notions like love, humility, and family. If you look at all of the violence in the media, you will see that the first is more real than the latter."

I wasn't too sure where this kid was going with his story, but at least he had gotten my attention.

"As a kid, family was my modern American fantasy. All the kids in my class seemed to have some version of a family. They all seemed to have at least one parent that loved them. I didn't."

Jonathan explained that he grew up in the foster care system. He had been shuffled from one bad home to the next. By the age of twelve he had given up on finding a loving family, and thought that loving parents were as much as a fantasy as vampires.

"Then I moved in with a new family, the Ryders," Jonathan continued. "They were different than the other families. They seemed to really want me. Unfortunately, by this time I still didn't think that it was possible to have a real family. I figured the parents couldn't possibly be as loving as they seemed, so I set out to prove this to myself."

I listened intently as Jonathan described everything that he did to prove that his foster parents didn't love him. He described years of drug abuse and parties. Then Jonathan ended his tale with the following.

"No matter how hard I tried to make the Ryders stop loving me, they didn't. The more I tried to push them away, the more I couldn't. Then one day I stopped trying. When I was seventeen, I asked the Ryders to adopt me, and they did. They showed me that family is not a modern American fantasy after all."

I smiled as Jonathan walked to his seat. His true story had certainly been a more interesting fantasy than everyone else's.

Date: Mar. 21, 2014
Category: Fiction
Author: Kate Redford
The Prompt: Flowers for Ann

Flowers for Ann flashes through my mind
rapidly, repeating every few seconds and then
stops quickly. My eyes rest on the bouquet in the
crystal-cut glass pitcher. I smile as I take in the
full scene.

Just after dawn I strolled along the garden
path. The blooms danced and dipped in the
gentle breeze while the dew glistened on their
petals. Gleefully they begged to be cut. I gently
place in my baskets a few reds, some yellows.
Then, I spotted a Helleborus named Amber Gem.
The ivory colored bloom is yellow in the center
and then blushed with rose along its edges. The
beautiful flower almost jumped right into the
basket.

Almost finished, I walked toward the cluster of
hardwood and nut trees. Didn't know what I was
looking for until I spotted some deep broadleaf
fern just beginning to unfurl. I picked several
spikes and placed them gently in the basket.
Turning toward the sunnier side of the garden I
looked for sprigs with arching tiny limbs and lots
of dainty flowers to complete my selection. Soon I
found some that were icicle blue, pale pink and
soft white in color. I quickly picked a few of each
and turned toward home.

My steps were light as I began to imagine in my mind the arrangement that would be created and the joy I would have in pulling it together. When finished I was not disappointed. I began to have pangs of regrets having made the bouquet to be given away. The flowers were so pretty and spoke to my soul.

Quickly I thought of a solution and gathered all the supplies I needed. Before long, after many an admiring glance, it was nearly finished. I picked up the thin, small brush with extra-long bristles and twirled them around and around in the oil.

The words "Flowers for Ann" flowed through my mind rapidly and repeatedly. The words "Flowers for Ann" flowed down my arm and through the brush as I swiftly reproduced them on the painting thus naming it "Flowers for Ann." Happiness and joy fill the air. The flowers were a gift for Ann in a painting and a gift for me in the arrangement in the cut glass pitcher.

Date: Jan. 8, 2014
Category: Fiction
Author: Louis K. Broussard Sr.
The man...the woman - An Earthly Mystery

"Doctor Ingram, we have lifted the man from the crevasse and are in full recovery mode," the radio operator reported.

"Excellent, Commander Ivan, continue with the procedures in the recovery facility and keep me informed of the progress," ordered Dr. Ingram.

On the Siberian glacier, the temperature can hover at minus 50 degrees, and is one of the coldest places in the world. It was extremely difficult on man and machinery to operate under these conditions. The discipline of men in these conditions was imperative, and with this expedition's crew it was impeccable. They had to come to extract a frozen man who was discovered on a previous exploration. The "Iceman" had been frozen for centuries and the possibility of resurrecting the frozen man to life would be the most remarkable feat ever accomplished in human biology.

The ice-encased body rose upward as the noisy crane roared in the icy wilderness. The cable groaned and squeaked as it rolled over the pulleys and then wound around the winch.

"Stop," yelled the foreman as he held his arm skyward and clenched his fingers to form a fist. "Boom over," he ordered as he pointed to the flatbed deck of the snow-track. He held his hand to a halt position and then directed the ice block down to the track's bed. The loaded vehicle drove to the Quonset hut. With a press of a remote, the roll-up door opened for their entrance. As the door closed behind the track, a large powered gurney was driven next to the track bed. The load was slid onto the gurney and guided through another set of doors and into the recovery room. Now a team of specialists was waiting for the iceman to begin the planned recovery.

In the first phase a dome fabricated of metal and Plexiglas was lowered over the frozen block of ice and man. All flex hoses were attached and a valve opened to fill nitrogen into the dome. This procedure flushed all air out through the exhaust valve. The nitrogen gas within the dome was gently heated raising the temperature and thus creating a controlled thaw. Phase two of the procedure began with a probe inserted into the abdomen of the man to monitor its progress. "It will be 24 hours before we fill the dome with oxygen and begin to resuscitate the Iceman," Commander Ivan said. "The monitors will automatically do their job so we can plan our work for tomorrow and get our well-earned rest."

The Iceman lay in the dome thawing slowly to the mean temperature of 33 degrees. If this body had been rapidly frozen hundreds of years ago, scientists believed the blood would be preserved to live again in the awakened body. The man was clothed in garments of woven fabric which looked

Egyptian but could be Mayan, but his features looked more Nordic than Mayan or Egyptian. Around his neck was a golden, twisted wire lanyard that held a mysterious medallion with strange inscriptions. The inscriptions were from an unknown source. The round medallion was over an inch thick and six inches in diameter with a faceted green gemstone in its center. What happened next will make us wonder about many mysteries hidden deep into the past.

As time passed and the crew slept, the temperature in the dome and the man reached the desired temperature of 33 degrees. Suddenly the green gemstone in the middle of the medallion began to glow brightly and other stones of red and blue began to glow and blink. The blinking was not random but in some kind of binary code. Perhaps the medallion was sending transmissions not understood by us. Suddenly the recovery room became blindingly bright as with a million candle power. It was being emitted from a wide beam of light that encircled the dome. It seemed to have a fog within the beam that swirled like smoke rising in a motion of a vortex. Suddenly the room became dark when all the electric power supply shut down. Just as quickly as the bright light had come it suddenly left and the power was restored. The dome which held the Iceman had vanished. Alarms blared and red warning lights flashed and this roused the resting crew. They came into the recovery room and stood in awe and confusion. They began to process the evidence to bring some explanation to what had occurred.

"Doctor Ingram, Doctor Ingram, come in please. Do you read? Come in please!" the voice of Commander Ivan on the radio was emphatic. There was a pause and then an answer from the doctor.

"I am here. What seems to be the problem, Ivan? I can tell in your voice that something has gone very wrong."

Ivan replied, "I am in shock, for the Iceman disappeared! Not only him but the recovery dome as well. All has totally vanished without a trace. Our guards were posted at all exits and the only noted anomaly was the power failure followed by the triggered alarms. There has to be an explanation but we have not yet found it. I am looking for answers."

"Ivan, did you check the surveillance cameras?" asked the doctor.

"I checked the camera and there was something strange on the one which focused on the recovery dome," Ivan began to speak with a tone of dismay. "The Iceman had a golden medallion around his neck. We could see it through the ice that covered his chest. The strange medallion on the Iceman, well...it began to glow and blink just before the bright lights appeared. The camera could not show anything with the light so intense. Suddenly the power went off and there was complete darkness for perhaps a minute. As soon as the lights returned the dome and contents were gone."

"Ivan, you must send me the tape of the recovery room camera. I need to study it for myself. I'll get back with you after I have seen it for myself," said Doctor Ingram.

In a distant galaxy, a spaceship orbited a planet in a parking orientation. On board the ship and in the Captain's quarters, was a celebration and homecoming. A crew member has recently returned after an absence of 2,000 years. He had been on a mission in the Milky Way galaxy on the blue planet earth.

"Here, here! the captain has words to say on our hero's return," announced the captain's first mate.

"Thank you Vanguard II for your service on the mission to earth. You have accomplished much with the Mayans and the Egyptians. You have persevered in an environment which is very different from ours. You gave the people teachings that enabled them to advance to a much higher level than if they lingered on their own. I am sure to this day the peoples of earth are mystified over the signs that they see which your teachings have left behind. So Vanguard, we raise our arm and salute you," the Captain said while motioning to the crew to join him.

On earth the pyramids in Egypt point skyward and offer questions but few answers. Elsewhere, on the other side of the earth are the Aztec and Inca ruins. A tourist observing these magnificent stone structures might say to his fellow tourist, "I guess only heaven knows the how and the why."

Date: Nov. 26, 2013
Category: Fiction
Author: Kate Redford
The Prompt: Hidden Camera

In my current world the Hidden Camera is everywhere! No longer am I able to hide from the continuous stare. The Hidden Camera dwells near the bank tellers and the gasoline pump. The lens glistens in the sunlight. So common I don't notice.

At the sporting events and the grocery stores the Hidden Camera is there. Embedded in places I miss seeing in my quick glance. The Hidden Camera is even with the teenager standing across the street on the corner.

I am unaware until my son says, "Mom your photo is in our school newspaper."

The Hidden Camera can be many different images. A rose bud, a ring on the pinky, a cigarette lighter or impressive gold bracelet. The Hidden Camera can be most elegant as a black onyx fountain pen placed in the breast pocket of a fine tailored silk suit. The Hidden Camera is easy to use and return to its resting place. With a flick of the wrist or sly movement of the hand the picture is taken.

Such is life in 2013. The Hidden Camera is everywhere. We trust no one and suspect everyone. When I step through the door with a smile on my face and a flick of my wrist, I bid farewell.

My day will be great with or without the Hidden Camera which is everywhere.

Date: Oct. 29, 2013
Category: Fiction
Author: Debbie M. Soileau
The Prompt: Odds Are...

Odds are he won't realize his mistake until I am long gone. By that time, his career will be over and he will be lucky to get his old job back. And I will be sitting on the lap of a man that appreciates a good woman, a man that just happens to have more time and money than he knows what to do with.

Poor Richard, he won't even know what happened.

Richard and I met when he was deputy sheriff of Podunk Hole, Mississippi, population 2,400. I failed to make a complete stop at the one stop sign in town and Richard came after me, lights flashing and siren blasting like I was on the FBI's Most Wanted list.

He walked up to my jeep and I was hit with his megawatt smile. Naturally, he wrote me a ticket. I accepted with a smile and an apology. Then he asked if I would like to get a cup of coffee. Me being me, I said "Sure, why not?" All the while I was thinking of that incredible smile and being at the epicenter of it.

We met at Dolly's Diner. He talked about wanting more out of life than being just a deputy sheriff. As I listened, I realized that he had the charm and smile that it would take to make it in politics. But he sorely lacked the mental ability to swim with the sharks. We talked until Dolly's closed and Richard asked if we could see each other again. Mind racing, possibilities evolving, I readily accepted his date.

Our relationship was on fast-track, marrying after four months of dating. We were both tired of being alone. He greedily drank my advice. He went with every suggestion. The next day was the same and I realized that Richard was a good deputy sheriff, but a poor senator. I knew I would have so much work to do on all major issues that he would be involved in.

My days were filled with answering his incessant questions and deep digging in the courthouse files figuring out answers to keep Richard on top.

One afternoon I decided to surprise Richard with a visit. I quietly knocked on his door and received no answer to enter, so I walked in. To my surprise and horror, Richard's creamy behind was doing the mamba with an unknown female. At first I just stood there and watched, not sure if what I was really seeing was happening. I have no idea how long I stood there because I was not noticed until after they each heard a sigh of relief. She was the first to notice me and modestly tried to cover her perfect body with her petite hands. Her mouth opened in disbelief, which made Richard turn around.

"Shelly, what are you doing here?" His voice was calm and he flashed that smile to try and throw me off guard.

"Well," I said, "I came to surprise you but it looks like you turned the tables on me." I was seething inside and my exterior was the proverbial calm before the storm. My mind was running rampant, revenge was the reason.

"Shelly, this is my legal aide, Jessica." He nonchalantly pulled up his pants, tucked in his shirt, zipped up and buckled his belt. Then he had the nerve to come towards me as if he wanted to hug me.

"Richard, I saw it all. Do you think I am a complete moron? Do you think I want you touching me after you have been with Little Miss Plastic Surgery?"

Jessica was dressed. "What do you mean, Little Miss Plastic Surgery? I am natural, from head to toe."

I couldn't help myself. I laughed until snot ran out of my nose. Only a man would not be able to see the fake lashes, the natural lavender eyes, the perky nose, and the lips that no woman except Angelina Jolie sported naturally. Not to mention, I got a look at her perfect figure and I could actually see the implants in her rear end.

"Come on, honey. You can fool men but you certainly cannot fool me. Odds are, there is nothing natural about you, except maybe your feet."

Richard stepped in front of me, uncertain of his next move. I looked deep into his eyes and saw remorse and embarrassment for his folly. I had to wonder just how many follies he had engaged in. I turned and calmly walked out his office door.

That was two years ago. As I sit in the airport lounge with my fiancé, I look back on Richard and how I had worked so hard to get him to the state capitol. I didn't regret it. It was certainly a learning experience for me. I knew that he was just a stranded seal that would be food for the sharks. Sure enough, he lost his seat not long ago. He just didn't have politics in his blood. Odds are, he went back to his job as deputy sheriff in Podunk Hole, Mississippi, population 2,400.

All I can say is, poor Richard, and yay me!

Date: Sept. 24, 2014
Category: Fiction, Short Stories
Author: Louis Broussard
The Prompt: Turning into Silence

The final attachment of silk threads sealed the inside wall, turning into silence the cocoon for which the chubby caterpillar would be forever changed. Let me explain how our little worm came to be here in this small measure of time.

Mr. McDonald loved to work in his garden and everyone who drove by would honk their horns and wave and smile. It was a pleasure and a joy for him, but as people drove by it appeared to them as work. His cabbages grew in a nice straight row and with the help of compost, fertilizers, and water as they grew dark green and luscious.

The beautiful garden was spied by a lovely butterfly. She had been flying through the gardens, fence rows, and fields, flying freely as a bird. It was love at first she beheld the row of cabbages. As she flittered she zigged and zagged with a precision only another butterfly could appreciate. She then landed on just the right leaf where she began to lay little white eggs and attached them under the leaf. The eggs were thus out of sight of wrens and sparrows and shaded from the hot sun rays. In a very short time the eggs hatched and out crawled little white worms one of which we will name Junior. Junior grew rapidly as he feasted on the luscious tender cabbage leaves. Junior had siblings nearby munching and chewing and chewing and munching. Their conversations were mostly misunderstood as they talked with their mouths full.

Junior asked, "Hello there, how is the weather on your edge of the leaf?" His neighbor was only two inches away. Two inches to the tiny caterpillar is like two miles to humans.

It answered, "It's a bit warm," munch, chew, "but the clouds help when they cast their shadows over me." Munch, munch, munch!

When the cool of the evening arrived, Junior went to work doing what caterpillars are designed to do; eat until its skin is as tight as a drum and is about to explode. He never explodes because his skin stretches like a balloon. As Junior lay attached to the underside of a big cabbage leaf, he received an internal message, a voice from deep within his being. This is a message that only now we are beginning to understand. People have named it DNA. It is like a blueprint that living bodies have and are most complete when they follow the instructions that it directs.

His message said, "You have had enough to eat and it is time for you to travel." Junior listened to the voice and began to crawl. He crawled over five, six, seven rows in the garden and then crossed over a big timber at the garden's edge. He crawled even farther until he bumped into a huge tree. To Junior it was a tree, but to us it's a bush. Junior looked up at the trunk by lifting the head end of his long worm-like body.

"Why do I want to climb this tree?" he asked himself.

It was that voice from inside his being that gave him the messages. It said, "Crawl up and then out onto a branch." He crawled out onto the branch and the voice spoke again. "Stop here," it ordered, and Junior stopped. "Now hang onto the limb by your rear pair of legs and let all other legs hang free," it commanded.

Junior, without fear, followed the instructions just as you would do when teachers give directions. Junior was now looking down far below his perch. He viewed the earth many miles below. Of course it was only six feet in human measurements. Suddenly, the upside down hanging caused a strange shiver throughout his whole being. It began at one end and pulsed to the other end.

"It feels like a chill and I want to cover myself with a blanket," he thought. Nothing that people observe can tell us what teaches a baby spider to weave a web for the first time, and nothing we can see that teaches a caterpillar to spin a silk covering around itself called a cocoon.

Junior felt a liquid accumulate at his mouth and instinctively began to attach this on the bark of the branch near his back legs. The silk glands in his mouth oozed the clear spittle that immediately dried into the silk thread when it is touched by the air. The silk threads formed a little house for Junior that we call a cocoon. It would be a shelter from the chills of fall and the ice of winter. Junior kept spinning and turning, twisting and tipping, and before long there was a smooth wall that surrounded him for his magical transformation. With the spinning of the last silk thread, Junior could not hear the busy noises of the outside world.

Date: Aug. 27, 2013
Category: Fiction, Short Stories
Author: Ashley Burleigh
The Prompt: Nice Bully
Title: Mandie

"Nice Bully? What do you mean, she was a nice bully?" Cherie asked.

"I'm just saying she was nice sometimes," I said, trying to find something kind to say about Mandie, not wanting to talk bad about a girl who had died. She was mean, but she couldn't defend herself.

"She was horrible, I'm not going to sugarcoat it just because she died."

"Did you know Mandie Hebert?" Shellie asked.

I grimaced as I imagined the horrible things Mandie must've said about me. I was tired of her starting rumors about me.

"Yeah, I hate her and if she died I wouldn't care."

"Um...Mandie died?"

I couldn't believe the words I heard. She must be talking about another Mandie. She was only seventeen.

"A drunk driver killed her."

As I hung up the phone, a wave of guilt overtook me. I hadn't meant what I said. I didn't want Mandie to die, but felt like I was responsible for her death, somehow. I was plagued with nightmares about Mandie.

"You wanted me to die. I'm dead now. Are you happy?" Mandie whispered in my dreams.

I woke up in a cold sweat, shouting, "I'm sorry," but I knew she couldn't hear me. I wondered if I should attend the funeral. What would I say if someone asked me if we were friends? We weren't friends.

I decided to go. I thought attending the funeral would give me closure. When I went up to the casket, I did not see a mean girl. I saw a young girl whose life was stolen, a girl who would never be able to attend her graduation, which she had missed by a week. I saw a girl who no longer had a future. My heart broke for her. I felt a lump in my throat, as her family mourned for her.

After the funeral, I still wrestled with guilt. I started hearing her home life had been difficult. Her dad had been abusive to her. Perhaps this was why she was so mean to everyone. I knew what I needed to do.

Two weeks after Mandie's death, I arrived at her gravesite. I placed a flower at her grave, and began to read a letter I wrote to her.

"Mandie, you're probably wondering why I'm here. We weren't friends. I wish we could have been. Maybe you needed a friend. I'm sorry for what I said about you. I didn't mean it, and I wish you were still here. I forgive you. I forgive you for the way you treated me and I understand why you did."

As I read those words the guilt left me. Then I began to think of all the bullies in school who made my life miserable. I wondered what they had been going through to make them act the way that they did. I dropped to my knees and I prayed for every single girl who had bullied me.

Date: July 30, 2013
Category: Fiction Poetry
Author: Bob Boese
The Prompt: Limericks

The limerick packs laughs anatomical
Into space that is quite economical
But the good ones I've seen
So seldom are clean
And the clean ones so seldom are comical
(ALL YOU NEED TO KNOW FOR THE FOLLOWING
IS THAT AN EVIL VOODOO PRIEST IS A BOKOR...)
The story is told that a bokor
saw a girl whose complexion was ochre.
He was sure it was better
to bed her than wed her
and determined to get her and poke her.
All his plans she was certain to dash
cause her business was loving for cash.
While his scheme was direct
what he couldn't expect
was the way that she gave him a rash.
To the medic he needed to travel
when his voice became courser than gravel.
He was scared that the swelling
was clearly not telling
how his future began to unravel.
And as for the end of this caper
both the jewels that surrounded his taper
were remarkably green
as he never had been
with the texture of old crumpled paper.

Date: June 22, 2013
Category: Fiction
Author: Louis K. Broussard Sr.
The Prompt: If I were President....
Title: My Fellow Americans

Indeed, if I were President of the U.S.A
I would declare all Mondays a care holiday
Not that I deplore this beginning week day
Not because I want to have my own way
But these gifts of freedom must have a say
Monday would be our freedom's time
It is a time to surrender the wants of self
A time of sharing our many ways to care
Doing for others frees a storehouse of wealth
It is for we who are blessed with good health
Our many nursing homes house the aged
We accept that lonely has meager comforts
Their silent pain is logged on clipboard pages
But our caring hands will fit warmly in theirs
Like rain that drains away so it is with cares
When a fire consumes the house is lost
A home is disrupted and faith may be tossed
People pose the question, "Where can we turn?"
Our actions are more useful than just concern
Let us prove that within, our faith does burn
If I were the President of the U.S. of A.
I would speak everywhere for freedom's way
We must try to love each other keeping no score
Practice loving those in need will open a door
Pass it forward, North, South, and shore to shore

Stand by your neighbors in times of tribulation
Know well that death receives no invitation
And conclude that sorrow is owned by none
For spiritual peace exceeds all our understanding
When our healing or your neighbor's has begun
You may grow a garden and share the fruits
You may plant flowers or mow lawns for the lame
Relinquish older clothes and help the needy
We will do all these things but not for the future
We will do these things to help change the game
Around us are those who live like hermit souls
They neither work, nor share, or give of
themselves
There are others who feel victimized and defeated
When they will see our Monday care day repeated
And our burning desire to love will be seeded
If I cannot be the President of the U.S. of A.
Let me try to do these things I thankfully pray
To find ways to lessen myself is to righteously live
A Monday is good but each day is even better
This is what I would do recorded here in this
letter.

Date: May 28, 2013
Category: Fiction
Author: Louis Broussard
The Prompt: Inside of An Egg

I climbed the many cement steps which were inlaid with colorful tiles. On the surface of each step were tiles of bird paintings. Perhaps they resembled some other kind of fowl. On the veranda I stood before a large mahogany door with ornate brass handles and hinges. Holding a small priceless package in one hand, with my free hand I knocked but made only a little sound. I spied the brass knocker that resembled a crowing rooster's leg and "let it fly," so to speak. It made a resounding knock that echoed on the other side of the door. I did not know what or who would answer, but I was prepared. I was packing my military 45 automatic pistol and my energy was focused on whom or what would answer the door.

The door knob began to turn and then the big door slowly opened to partially expose a gorgeous dame. She appeared to me as someone out of 'Cave Man Magazine'. She had an inquiring look on her face which compelled me to speak. I said, "Miss, please excuse the interruption but I have come to deliver a package to a person at this address. The name has been smudged by the rain and I can only read the name Frances. I'm just a courier and I am only trying to do my job, Miss."

"Won't you please come in Mr___?"

She waited for me to fill in the blank. "Thank you Miss, for it's a bit damp and chilly out here." She still had that inquiring look. "My name is J.B. Snoop, but most people call me Fred."

She grinned and opened the door wide and motioned for me to enter. I removed my fedora and she took it from me. I could not help but notice the tattoo on the back of her dainty white hand. It looked like, well, some kind of chicken! I was removed from that thought when she said, "Follow me, Fred, and I'll see if I can help you accomplish your mission."

She led me into a large room with vaulted ceilings of ornate plaster works. In the center of the ceiling was the largest glass chandelier I had ever seen. I stood on the marble floor which glistened under the lights. I then noticed I was standing in the home's art gallery. Around the room hung expensively framed art work. It was then I noticed that all of the paintings had chickens in them. "Strange," I thought to myself, "there isn't one rooster in any of these paintings."

She startled me when she said, "Are you coming, Mr. Fred?" As she led me into the library her spiked heels made clicking echoes throughout the rooms. "Please have a seat here," she said as she motioned toward a large overstuffed chair covered in tapestry. You guessed it, of chickens. Sitting down, I placed the package on my lap and gave her my full attention. She cordially asked, "Fred, would you like some hot eggnog? It is special, you know. It is made with eggs freshly laid in bedroom number 26."

"No, thank you. I have an allergy to eggs," I said, all the while trying to act disappointed. "Miss, I would now like to meet this Frances, if you don't mind."

"Why, of course you would," she said "and you have, for I am Frances de la Chick. I am the sole heir to the Poulle estate that is quite immense."

"Yes, now that you mention it, I have read about it. It was in 'Who is Who in the World of Wealth' magazine. Your picture and an article about your jewels were featured. I'm sorry to confess, I only browsed the article." I looked about the library and realized nearly all of the books had something to do with poultry, chickens, hens, etc. It was a fowl library indeed!

Suddenly my eyes fell upon Frances and our eyes met intensely. She parted her moistened, luscious lips and spoke softly, "Are you going to give me my package?" "Yes Miss Frances, but here," and I removed from the inside pocket of my coat a receipt. "Please sign this form," I said. "This is standard procedure and this will release me from this responsibility." I slipped the cap off my black Bic pen and while smiling, handed it and the form to her. She signed it F. Chick, and gave it to me. She hastily tore off the wrapping paper and opened the box.

There was tissue stuffing which protected the object. She expressed extreme delight by squealing loudly and then making a strange clucking sound as she lifted a bejeweled, sparkling egg. I could only say, "It is the most beautiful Fabergé piece I have ever seen!"

Frances held it in her white-skinned tattooed hands and said, "I wonder what is inside the egg?" Her luscious lips began to tremble and two large tears beaded and trickled down her rosy cheeks. "My father...left this...for me," she stammered while opening the two piece egg. She held between her thumb and forefinger a beautiful diamond pendant. "Unbelievable," I said to myself. It was in the shape of a baby chicken. Frances sniffed and then said, "My father called me his little chick. Easter is tomorrow and it so happens to be on my 21st birthday. I will then be fully in charge of the estate. What more could a girl ask for, Fred?"

I blurted out, "A chick mobile?" I left Frances de la Chick to live a fowl life. I had this thought: "Inside the egg was a well-hatched plan for a Chick that deserves no less."

Date: Apr. 30, 2013
Category: Fiction
Author: Charlene Morella
The Prompt: Hello coffee...
Title: Flavor of Friendship

Hello Coffee. Here we are again staring at the CC's drink menu on the wall. The selections never vary but we look at it as if a new coffee flavor might mysteriously appear with flashing neon lights saying, 'Drink me!'

"What are you having, Lucia?" I ask.

"I think I'll have a tall Mochasippi. I didn't have time to eat. This is my supper. What are you having, Glenva?"

"I want a tall café latté—no paper cup, please. Could I have a cup and saucer?" I don't like drinking out of a tiny slit in the top of a paper cup.

"Yes, ma'am," says the young lady behind the counter. "And you, ma'am?" she inquires.

"I'll have a tall regular coffee with soy milk."

My choice seldom varies, compliments of lactose intolerance and inability to digest a lot of sugar. I don't mind. It isn't the coffee that's the big draw for these coffee klatches, but the cherished time of three good friends being together. If we are lucky, we manage to meet for coffee once every two or three weeks. If one of us is unavailable, we don't congregate until all three of us can make it. No one wants to miss out on catching up, the good laughs, the shoulders to cry on, or the juicy gossip.

It's an unwritten rule that we each get equal time for chit-chatting. It also goes without saying that if any one of us is in the midst of some life-crisis and needs the consoling of two good friends who never judge, and the catharsis that only validation and gentle, loving advice can provide–then our private coffee shop podium is theirs for the evening.

When our evening escapades to our favorite java joint last for as long as two and half hours, our husbands have learned not to worry. They know we never run out of things to talk about. The three of us have known each other more than twenty years. We have watched each other's kids grow up, get married, and have kids of their own. We have been there for each other through turbulent times and moments when hilarity reigned supreme. We have helped each other out with garage sales, graduation parties, unloading U-Haul trucks, serious car accidents, cooking meals, getting to doctor's appointments, and cleaning up after hurricanes.

We have borrowed from one another clothes, dishes, air mattresses, children's toys, plant cuttings, prescription medicine, electrical tools, pickup trucks, and good books. We've held each other's hands through life threatening illnesses, crisis in our children's lives, the caretaking of our elderly parents, and the ultimate funerals of that generation that came before us. We pray for each other constantly and there is nothing we wouldn't do for each other.

We have been known to allow our husbands into our inner sanctum. In fact, for most occasions, we encourage their presence—just not our evening coffee klatches. They have their own brand of quality time together. It's known as eighteen holes of golf with a beer and hamburger after. In fact, the Ya-Yos, the name we've given to our spousal group, get along so well.

The six of us are very compatible and have shared many nights out on the town, quiet dinner parties in each other's homes, birthday celebrations too numerous to count, and golfing trips in three states.

Our memories may fade when it comes to the countless moments we have spent together, but the loving history these moments have created among best friends will never fade. It's like the chocolate syrup on top of a Mochasippi, or the whipped cream on top of a café latté, or the cinnamon sprinkles on a coffee with soy milk. It's the flavor of friendship that brings the indelible aroma and the marvelous aftertaste to everything we shared and savored in life.

Date: Mar. 26, 2013
Category: Fiction
Author: Ashley Burleigh
The Prompt: Some people called the child
precocious, while others call him a straight up
brat...
Title: Skylar the Brat

Some people called the child precocious, while
others called him a straight up brat. Apparently,
my child was now calling him her new best friend.
Skylar and his family had been our neighbors
since we moved into the neighborhood three
years ago, but I had never invited him over to
play with Maddy, because of the horror stories I
had heard about him from other parents. Then
one day she came home from school declaring to
me that Clara was not her friend anymore and
Skylar was her new best friend. I was not too
worried about this at first. Maddy had been
friends with Clara since preschool, and I thought
this whole "Skylar is my new best friend" thing
was just a phase, but a month later Maddy was
still coming home from school talking about her
new best friend Skylar.

"I thought that this whole disapproving of her
friends thing was supposed to happen at sixteen
years old, not six years old." I sighed to my
husband.

"That's not the point. Maddy is such a good
kid. She's got perfect conduct in school, and I

have heard stories about this kid. I don't want him to get her into trouble."

"If you're so worried about it, why don't you just invite him over to play with Maddy? That way you can get to know the child before you immediately decide he is terrible."

"I guess so." I rolled my eyes knowing my husband was right, but not wanting to admit it.

When I told Maddy that Skylar would be coming over after school to play she was, of course, a lot more excited about it than I was.

"Yay, mommy, I can't wait! I'm so excited. This is great."

"Yeah, really great," I said, glad that Maddy did not quite get sarcasm.

From the moment that Skylar walked into the door, I could see where the terms precocious and brat could describe him.

"Mrs. Sherrie, you would be really pretty if you wore makeup. My mom has some you can borrow. I can bring it over next time I come to play," he had said. I couldn't believe I had seriously just been insulted by a six year old.

"Give him a chance, Sherrie, he's six. He doesn't mean to be rude." My husband said that after I complained to him how much of a brat Skylar really was.

The next day Maddy came home in tears. I was certain that Skylar must have said something to upset her, but when I asked her what happened she said that Clara stole her pink hair bow and that Skylar stuck up for her. "He's a good best friend, Mommy," she had said. I still was not so convinced.

"That was really nice of him," I said thinking maybe Skylar wasn't so bad.

"Can Skylar come play tomorrow after school?"

I reluctantly agreed. When Skylar came over, I baked cookies.

"Thank you so much for the cookies. My mommy doesn't have time to bake me cookies, because she works too much. These are the best cookies I have ever had," he said, handing me a flower he picked outside. That was when I realized that Skylar was not as bad as I thought he was. Maybe he was a little bit precocious, but he was not a brat.

Now Maddy is nine years old. Skylar and Maddy are still best friends, and I am glad they are. Skylar is such a good friend to Maddy. He always looks out for her in school, and he is like a son to me. I am so glad that they are friends because Skylar taught me a valuable lesson. He taught me to never judge anyone based on what people say and to always get to know a person before I judge them.

Date: Jan. 28, 2013
Category: Fiction
Author: Louis Broussard
The Prompt: After the ball drops...
Title: Hope Springs Eternal

As the ball dropped on New Year's Eve, my alarm buzzed annoyingly waking me from a restful slumber. I reached out for the alarm while keeping my eyes closed. I had done this act many times before in my dark room. The strobe light reflections on the wall drew my eyes to look at the images on my muted Cyclops. I had left the T.V. on for viewing this event of midnight madness which was presently unfolding before my eyes. I unmuted the control and listened to the announcer say, "5,4,3,2,1, Happy New Year.....!!!!"

As the camera panned the cheering crowd of jubilant humanity, all of which were missing their chance for restful sleep, I mentally shook my head cynically. At this time of the night Scrooge had nothing I couldn't match, and missing my sleep had its way to promulgate my propensity for acidic cynicism. The gazillions of jubilant participants I surmised were juiced up by the adrenalin flowing through their hypertensive vessels, or perhaps it was the alcohol they had consumed.

There were still other people who had a deep abiding need to be totally and insanely crazy in this celebratory moment. I thought that their escape was perpetrated by the fall of the crystal ball. The truth is that reality had no part in this joyful insanity.

Bills and mortgages, sickness or health, wealth or poverty, and any other detraction had no place with this intersection of time and space. As far as east is from west, a great divide was catalyzed by a force field brought to the here and now by the falling ball. My T.V. remote only required the slight pressure of my opposing thumb to kill the one eyed Cyclops.

The room became comfortingly dark as I closed my eyes. I took a deep breath hoping to re-enter my encounter with the sandman at Neverland. Boom!. Boom!. Pop!...Boom, crackle, crackle, crackle! Noooo, I said to myself, for it would be impossible to shut out the noise of the fireworks and the resulting explosions. It seemed that my neighbors had produced a community war zone.

I decided to slip into my robe and observe from my front porch all the hard earned wages as they were rocketed into the sky and burned into a momentary burst of bright lights and booms before falling to the earth as spent ash. The rockets' red glare and bombs bursting in air gave proof to me that dreams are not only for the sleeping but for the wakeful, "the truly living."

The "oohs" and "aahs" from the wide-eyed children, both the young and old, the rich and poor, and somehow the unfolding events were infectious. The infectious insanity entered into me so that I too caught the dream. I suddenly realized that tomorrow always has the unknowns at its center, but right now we are in the present. This is the place where the past begins and the future meets my next breath. This is where living takes place, and the ball that dropped is now metaphorically dropping with every breath I take, offering me a moment to celebrate.

The bombs bursting before my eyes into multicolored neon bright sparkles, is the symbol of the effervescent spirit of the human character (heart). I surmised that this is not a right brain or left brain thing. No, it is the seed of hope that springs eternal in the heart of man.

My sleep will happen later, but right now I want to be really awake! I said to myself, "Happy New Year!"

Date: Dec. 2012
Category: Fiction
Author: John Francois
The Prompt: Santa rethinks his life...

First of all, Santa hated snow. He hated the icy cold. He hated driving that drafty sleigh year after year on Christmas Eve. It was way too small for all the stuff he had to carry, anyway. There were too many children. And speaking of children, he was sad to say, he'd grown to hate them.

They weren't the same anymore. Children had evolved from sweet, innocent little creatures who had once been happy with a doll or a wooden horse, nice little gender specific toys, to where they cried and whined and fought over presents like video games that taught them how to kill. They wanted things like iPads and iPods and Smartphones and CD players, stuff he'd never even imagined a hundred years ago.

Oh, yes. Today's children were self-centered little monsters, brought up to think that Christmas was a time for them, not for religious reflection. Well, what else could you expect, them growing up like that? He had a belly full of the whole "Santa Claus is coming to town" thing.

If Xmas was supposed to be a time for giving, then he would give his reindeer a rest. Give his elves a rest. He would burn his list of who was naughty and who was nice. He really didn't care anymore, because the deportment of the kids was no longer his responsibility. It was time to dump these duties squarely on the parents, where they rightfully belonged. Of course, some parents would not accept this. They would simply turn around and pass that accountability on to the schools, the churches and government social services.

Yep, time to retire. Tired, tired he was. Good grief, he'd been at this game for almost two thousand years. And he would not retire at the North Pole, either. Who would want to live there? No cable TV, no garbage pickup?

He would move down to Mexico, to the sunny shores of Lake Chapala, a delightful little place just south of Guadalajara. And the first thing he'd do would be to shave off his stupid beard that made him look so old, then shed a few pounds.

And not only that. It was time for a new mate. His current wife, Nannook of the North, a simple Eskimo who preferred blubber and live maggots for a meal, well, that just wouldn't do for his new lifestyle. He'd find himself a little Mexican cutie. They would eat things like tacos and burritos and tamales, and enchiladas, and drink lots of margaritas on the beach!

Oh yeah!

One last "Ho, Ho, Ho," and one ringing "Bah and Humbug," and he was out of here.

Date: Nov. 27, 2012
Category: Fiction
Author: Ashley Burleigh
The Prompt: My life is made up of seconds...

My life is made up of seconds, many of them insignificant. Every now and then a friend comes into your life making the minuscule seconds in your life become significant. Staring into Mister Hanson's casket, I feel a tear drop run across my face, as I realize that I will never see Mr. Hanson again.

I remember when Mister Hanson moved next door to my apartment two years ago. I was nineteen and I thought I knew everything. Mister Hanson was seventy five years old, and he knew a lot more than I did. In my arrogance I viewed his wisdom as a nuisance.

Every morning when I left my apartment for my college classes, I would run into Mister Hanson in the hallway. Conveniently, he would leave his apartment the same time as me to take his Labrador on a walk. He always had a smile and a kind word to share with me. Actually, he had many kind words to share with me. At first I tried to avoid running into Mister Hanson. He always had a lot to say, and his conversations in the hallway often made me late for class. Not that I really wanted to attend my classes, but I knew that if I failed out of college in my third semester my family would think I was a total idiot. My older brother and sister both graduated from college with straight A's. I had to do the same.

Although I tried to avoid Mister Hanson, he was quite persistent and no matter what time I left my apartment to go to class he always managed to run into me. After some time I did not find his conversations with me to be a nuisance. I realized that he was very funny and he always had something interesting to say to me.

One morning I ran into Mister Hanson at four in the morning. I had just gotten home from a night of partying with my boyfriend Carlson and my best friend Trish. The party scene has never really been for me, but it is for Carlson and Trish, so I always tagged along. Watching Carlson flirt with every girl he saw and Trish get so high she had no idea what was going on, wasn't my idea of fun, but I didn't trust Carlson enough to let him go out without me.

"What brings you home so late?" Mister Hanson asked. He was obviously headed out somewhere ridiculously early.

"Um… I was studying with my friend Trish. We have a really rough test coming up in my history class." I lied. I knew my lie sounded really lame, and that Mister Hanson probably would not believe that I had been studying all night. However, I was beginning to value my friendship with Mr. Hanson and I did not think that he would approve of my activities.

I could tell that he didn't really believe me. I expected him to say something like, "You young

kids out partying, not taking anything seriously",
but instead he said, "History huh? I love history.
Why don't you come over this afternoon and I'll
help you study for your test."

The truth was I really could use the help in
studying and Mister Hanson was old so he
probably did know a lot about history, so I
agreed. I enjoyed my visit with Mister Hanson so
much that I began visiting him every week. I
enjoyed listening to his stories about his life and
how things were when he was my age. Even more
than that, I loved to hear him talk about his wife
Eva. His eyes always lit up when he talked about
how beautiful she was. He would tell me stories
about how they met and stories of his life with
her. He would say, "I can't wait till I see my dear
friend in heaven." I realized that Carlson never
looked at me the way Mister Hanson looked at
Eva, so I ended things with him. I stopped
hanging out with Trish and began making friends
in my classes that had the same interests as me.

I remember one day I told Mister Hanson that I
did not want to go to study business anymore. I
want to be an art teacher. My dad wants me to
help run the corporation he owns. Follow in his
footsteps; follow in my brother and sisters, but art
is my life. I want to teach it to others. He looked
at me and said, "Life is too short to try to waste it
making others happy. You should spend 24/7
doing the things that make you happy." The next
day I changed my major.

Two weeks later Mister Hanson knocked on my door. "I wanted to let you know that I am moving. My granddaughter is worried about me. She thinks I am getting old. She thinks I need looking after, but I will be the one looking after her. You know you remind me a lot of her," he had said.

One year later I had heard about his death. Placing a flower on his casket I know that he is with Eva in heaven looking down at me. "Thank you for being such a good friend," I say. "I can't wait to see you again in heaven."

Date: Oct. 30, 2012
Category: Fiction
Author: Cindy Bethel
The Prompt: The Cat Came Back

The cat came back. I couldn't understand it.
There was no reason for its second return. After
the first time I'd assumed it had been an error on
my part but now I knew this had to have been a
deliberate act. I'd double checked the address
twice this time and still here the package was
stamped 'Return to Sender' on the white
cardboard of the small rectangular box. I couldn't
help but hum the old Elvis tune to myself as I
turned the package once over in my hands. What
had been intended as a gesture of love and
friendship now frustrated me.

I picked at the corner of the packing tape and
after tearing the strip free began emptying the
Styrofoam packing peanuts onto my living room
floor. Shadow, my jet black kitten, began batting
them around the room and I was momentarily
distracted as I watched her spin in circles trying to
remove the one held by static electricity clinging
to her back.

Turning my attention back to the box in hand,
I lifted from the residual peanuts a well-worn
stuffed black cat that looked as though it had
been given one too many hugs in its life. There
was still a blob of glue circling the base of the
cat's tail from where my mother had saved the

day with her glue gun after the great rocking chair tragedy of '89. That was the day my daughter had named the stuffed cat Shadow, "cause his tail was hiding in the shadows when I pulled him" my daughter had told me. She had been inconsolable until grandma explained that kitties have nine lives and losing a tail surely can't count for more than just a half of one. This notion had soothed her sobs and brought a smile to my face as I recalled the great lengths grandma had taken to turn what normally would have been a one-minute task into a surgical production complete with dish towels tied around their mouths and socks over their shoes to make sure that no germs would compromise Shadow's health during the procedure. I could still hear them; "Glue stick." "Glue stick, check." "Glue gun." "Glue gun, check."

Shadow had seen a long and hard life. More trips through a washing machine and dryer than some of the clothes I own. I couldn't help but miss those times as I watched the stuffed cat's namesake batting at a hovering peanut caught in the draft from the floor vent. Those memories were some of my favorite. She and I, and of course, Shadow, had been inseparable. Two peas in a pod. Thick as thieves. And now, now even the postal service couldn't bring us together.
I held Shadow to my chest as I walked to the kitchen and lifted the receiver to my ear. I dialed her number as I held my breath. On each unanswered ring my heart sank a little more. I

had thought Shadow may have been able to mend the damage between us. That maybe an old friend could help us become new friends. Start over again, maybe.

No one was answering my call. Then I heard it, my daughter's sweet voice asking "Hello?" from the other end. I choked back the tears as I answered, "Happy Halloween, sweetie."

Date: Aug. 2012
Category: Fiction
Author: Ashley Burleigh
The Prompt: The 200 foot hemlock tree swayed gently in the early morning breeze...
Title: The Hemlock Tree

The two hundred foot hemlock swayed gently in the early morning breeze. I sighed knowing that this was probably the last time I would see the tree. Now that I was dead, I am also glad that I had specified that I had wanted my body buried underneath this tree. My great granddaddy planted that tree, and now it stood there baring its pine needles above its red bark. Momma loved that tree. We sat outside on many mornings like this drinking our coffee and listening to the birds perched in the trees. I promised momma that I was never going to chop down that tree, not that I would want to. The hemlock integrated itself into my family. Jimmy said that if I left him he would chop down the tree.

"Well, Momma, I found a way to keep the tree up and get away from Jimmy." I smiled.

You are probably wondering, if I am dead, how am I telling this story. Well, it's complicated. I'll tell you the story if you promise not to judge me. What we did was wrong, but it was the only way.

I married Jimmy underneath the hemlock tree when I was 21 years old. I could not think of a better place to get married than underneath that tree. The wedding was perfect, but I guess perfect weddings don't mean perfect marriages. I was a young naive girl and Jimmy promised me the world. Jimmy never did give me the world, but he did give me plenty of black eyes.

I'm surprised that Jimmy hadn't killed me. The first time he hit me was when we had only been married two weeks. It was because I had cooked something for dinner he did not like. At first, I thought I had imagined it. Especially, since he said, "I didn't hit you, I just touched you." But the violence got worst. One day he choked me so hard that I could barely talk for two weeks. He controlled where I went, who I talked to and even what I wore. You are probably wondering why I didn't just leave him. Trust me, I tried many times. He always cried and said it would never happen again. He even told me that he could not live without me and that if I left him, he would find me and kill me. I believed him. How couldn't I? Jimmy was a dangerous man. If he could choke me, couldn't he just as easily kill me?

Jimmy did not allow me to go anywhere without him. He was so certain that I would cheat on him. "You can't trust a fat tramp like you," he had said. I used to sneak out when he left for work. Every morning I walked, just to clear my head. For a moment I felt free. When I got back I would sit under the hemlock tree. I felt its pine needles sway above me, and I wanted to sway freely like the tree. I would sit under it and pray that God would give me the strength to leave Jimmy.

I met Thomas when I was on one of my morning walks. He greeted me with a smile and kind eyes. I told him right away that I was married because I did not want him to get the wrong idea. We became great friends. We began to meet up regularly to walk. We would talk about life in general and Thomas's work. He was a mortician, so his job was interesting. Sometimes after our walk we would sit under my hemlock tree and laugh. I never invited him in. I wasn't happy with Jimmy but I did not want to cheat. One day as we sat under the tree he looked at me with a concerned face and said, "Why don't you just leave him? You deserve better."

By better, I knew that Thomas meant himself, and I also knew that he was right. "I don't know what you mean." I denied it.

"Lizzie, don't lie to me. I know he hits you. I've seen all your bruises and your black eyes." He wiped my tears as I started to cry. He listened as I told him why I could not leave.

He held me and said "I have a plan. Do you trust me?"

I did trust him, so today we carried out his plan.

Thomas waited until he could get his hands on a body at the morgue that was close to my build and height. This morning he brought the body to my house decapitated. I don't know the details about how he obtained the body or where he put the head. I did not want to know. I got my husband's knife from his drawer. Thomas and I wore gloves. It was hard for me to cut myself, but I knew I needed to for the scene to look convincing. I cut my arms, my hands, my legs, my feet and watched as the blood leaked onto the floor. Thomas moved the body over the blood. I closed my eyes as Thomas stabbed the body with my husband's knife. I knew the body was already dead, but I still did not want to watch.

Now, I am watching the tree sway for one last time. I know Thomas and I have to leave quickly so no one sees us. Thomas knows how to make fake IDs and can access security card information, so I will now take on the identity of the dead girl. We plan on moving as far away as we can where no one knows either of us. Everyone in town knew that Jimmy was abusive. He will be charged with my murder and he will finally pay for everything he has done to me. Now that I am dead, I can finally live.

Date: July 31, 2012
Category: Fiction
Author: Cindy Bethel
The Prompt: Mary had been dead for a week...

Mary had been dead for at least a week. I had killed her with my own hands. Killed her without a second's thought to the long-term ramifications of my impulsive action. The instant it was over I felt shell shocked. My hands froze and my eyes couldn't focus on an image. Everything I had done the last five years had led me inexorably to this moment ... to her death. And now it was over. She was dead and I had killed her. Now what? What do you do when the one person in your life who has claimed so much of your time and devotion is suddenly gone? It's impossible to feel nothing when you steal the soul of a being who trusted you implicitly with their life.

Mary never saw it coming. Her days used to be filled with frolicking in the meadow behind the house and playing with the other children who lived next door. She was a free spirit and the sort of child that could warm the heart of even the crotchety old woman across the street. I had fallen in love with her energy from the first moment. She had been full of life and the kind of spunk only a child could have. And now she was gone.

The last seven days had dragged by at a snail's pace. I paced back and forth in the den, waiting for the call that never came. Jumping every time that there was a knock at the door. Did I do the right thing? I had to kill her, didn't I? I told myself there was no other way … that I had done what was necessary and that people would understand and forgive me. They would understand why I did it, why I had to do it. Still, I wasn't sure. If only I could turn the clock back, I would have done things differently. Maybe she didn't have to die; maybe there had been another way.

The phone's ring jarred me from my inner tug of war and sent my heart through my chest. Trying to calm myself and steady my voice, I lifted the receiver to my ear. "Hello?" I asked in a poor attempt at a casual greeting. "Jim? It's Dave. The publishers loved the manuscript you sent over last week. They want to go to print in a month. Boy, you outdid yourself this time! They loved when you killed off little what's-her-name."

Date: June 26, 2012
Category: Fiction
Author: Ashley Burleigh
The Prompt: The Hook...
Title: Kidnapped

Stacia opened her eyes, but darkness was all she saw. "Where am I? Am I dead? Am I still dreaming?" she thought. Stacia felt a sharp pain surging through her body. She realized that she was awake and not dreaming when she felt her head throbbing. She reached out to touch her head, and underneath her matted hair, she felt a bump on her head.

"What happened to my head? Did I fall?" she wondered. Stacia tried to move her body, but she could not move because she was trapped in a tight space. She squinted her eyes for an indication of her locale, but all she could see was a void of nothingness. She could smell a mixture of gasoline and musk. She could hear a muffled familiar sound, but she still could not see anything. When she finally was able to identify that familiar sound, she felt a sudden pain in her chest and her heart began to pound uncontrollably.

That's a car honking and cars passing by. Oh my God! I'm in the back of a trunk. Someone must have hit me on the back of the head and stuffed me in this trunk. I am going to die. I'm either going to suffocate in this trunk or whoever put me in here is going to kill me. I'm never going to see my girls again, or Isaac. "God, please get me out of here!" she cried. She felt her breath grow heavy in a fit of panic. When she thought about Isaac, a tinge of guilt began to surge her thoughts. She felt guilty about the argument they had had last night and that she had not apologized to Isaac. The argument was so silly. Why hadn't she apologized? Now, all she wanted to do was wrap her arms around him and say she was sorry. All she wanted was to see her husband and kids, but she probably would not be able to again.

Desperately, she felt for a latch on the trunk to get out, but she found none. She pounded on the trunk with her fist, until her arms and legs were so numb, that she could no longer move. Exhausted and defeated, she began to accept her fate.

"Who would do this?" she wondered, but deep inside she knew exactly who had done this to her. Suddenly, she heard silence and felt no movement. The car came to a stop, and she could hear footsteps, and the sound of someone opening the trunk. When she saw his face, her heart pounded in terror. "Hey, did you miss me?" a familiar voice piped."

Date: May 29, 2012
Category: Fiction
Author: John Francois
The Prompt: The Afternoon

The afternoon of my death was everything I had hoped for. Death had been hovering on my mountain top, and when I was ready for plucking, he came quickly. Having lived for 102 years, nine months and 22 days, I was prepared. Actually, I'd been ready since I was 90. After so many years of my wiggling presence on earth, I figured 90 was a good time to throw in the towel. By then, I'd lived a full life, left much good work behind, and had nothing to look forward to except lingering around waiting to die.

That was one thing I had learned. Don't hang around. Move on. Hop the next train, catch the next plane, and leave town. Begin again, start a new career, meet new people, try new things. I'd seen too many of my friends hesitate, then stay for an encore. They were miserable. When a party is over, people should leave. The band collects its instruments, you collect your coat, the host holds the door open and thanks you for coming. If you don't leave, you become an unpleasant irritant, like a strand of hair stuck on a bar of soap.

So at 90 and not dead, I sold everything I owned, bought a first class plane ticket and headed for Nepal. Don't ever let people tell you that you're too old to fly. Airline aides meet you at airports, smile at you, and with their wheelchairs roll you past immigration and custom lines to your next plane.

When I arrived in New Delhi, I took the train to Katmandu. Nepal is full of foreigners, mostly young people who go trekking the foothills of the Himalayas. Katmandu is no longer the "in place," as it had been, but it's still far enough away from the main path to draw the adventurous.

I found a rental agency that had exactly what I wanted: a rustic hut at the top of a nearby mountain which people could climb without too much difficulty. I let my hair and beard grow long, and established myself as a wise old seer who would enlighten anyone who comes searching for TRUTH.

And this is what I told them, my exact words: "Don't stay too long at the party." They waited for more. I said nothing else. They left, suitably mystified.

I was on that mountain top for 12 years before Death came looking. I left on a glorious afternoon while watching the slanting rays of the western sun tickle the tops of the snow-capped Himalayas in bursts of pinks and reds. Even Everest made a rare appearance, a mountain usually shrouded in clouds. A perfect afternoon to my life.

Date: Mar. 27, 2012
Category: Fiction
Author: Lori Peters
Without using a color word, describe a tree.
Title: For You

They all start out solid. Deep roots, a firm foundation. Settled and strong. Confident in where it is, what it is. Why it is.

But a solid base is just a trunk and a trunk is nothing without branches. Stability is wasted if it is not used to reach out. To touch the stars. To feel the wind and hear its whispers from everywhere, screaming that the world is big and smells like adventure.

And the branches can't be bare. They can't stand naked in the elements, depending on themselves to grow. Sunlight must be caught and drank and changed to energy. The leaves know that you can't take without giving, and you can't live without dying.

And their death is the most beautiful of all the life round them, because they knew how to live.

And when they fall, the old branches must face the world alone. And when the branches break, or are taken to be useful, and the trunk grows old and hollow, then I will hide my secrets inside for you to find.

You'll find them on the day you begin your adventure away from your solid base. When you finally decide to live your life brighter than all the world around you.

Date: Feb. 2012
Category: Nonfiction
Author: Charlene Morella

Title: Valentine Love Letter to My Husband...The Touch

My Darling Husband,

We had our first date forty-nine years ago and I remember it like it was yesterday–not because you were a handsome man, not because you were an excellent dancer, not even because you were one of the few boys that I knew who had a car on campus.

The year was 1961, we were juniors and you asked me out for the first USL football game. As we exited your car and headed for the stadium, you gently but deliberately, reached for my hand. I showed no hesitancy in accepting your gesture as we walked through the graveled parking lot. Your loving and protective touch told me so much about you. Electrifying was the only way to describe it. I knew that we were destined for a future together.

Holding hands has been a way of non-verbal communication between us for as long as I can remember; simply holding hands for a leisurely walk around the block, or reaching for each other while we watched TV.

Other times we reached for each other, holding on for dear life; receiving sad news that a beloved family member had passed away or listened to a doctor give us some bad news.

Other times were poignant moments we wanted to share as one; watching one of our children get married, or attending a grandchild's christening.

During our forty-seven years of marriage I have given you many titles: my mentor, my lover, wonderful father to our children, the guy that makes me laugh even when I'm trying to be mad at you, my best friend, but most of all, my hero. Caretaker is the latest title thrust upon you as I enter another cancer journey.

The event that brought us full circle in my archives of meaningful touches was one that you may not remember, as they have become so common-place as one of our love rituals.

My day had been like so many others; living in a fog, commandeered by chemotherapy, never knowing what was going to be the side-effect of the day–the week–the month. By bedtime I had convinced myself that I was a worthless, diseased blob ruining your life and mine.

You had a long day teaching your classes, taking care of the blob, and taking up the slack for the blob. No complaints from you–just smiles of encouragement and being a little bit of a buffoon to get me laughing.

As we went to bed, I reached for my headset to listen to my relaxation and healing tape in hopes that it would calm me and put me to sleep. In the darkness, I felt your finger tips overlap mine with the same gentleness of our first touch, but conveying more love and "white-knight protectiveness" than ever before. Again, I felt the sparks. I knew it was the strength you and God wanted me to receive.

My heart was aware of all of this as my body was lulled to sleep by the voice from my headset. As my tape came to an end, you removed it and placed it on the night stand. As tired as you were, you had kept yourself awake to do this one small task for me so that I did not have to be disturbed. I awoke refreshed and with a new attitude, ready to fight my opponent. I could do no less for the man that was fighting the good fight with me and for me.

There is no way to calculate how many hundreds of touches that we have shared since that first one. All I know is that each one represents a very deep and abiding love, giving strength and meaning to my life. I will never yield when adversity invades our lives, as long as you keep reaching out with those wonderful touches of yours. I will always take your hand and I will always offer you mine.

Your adoring wife,
Charlene

Date: Feb. 2012
Category: Nonfiction
Author: John Morella

Title: Valentine Love Letter to My Wife

Dear Charlene,

I met you forty-nine years ago in college and we have been married for forty-seven years. I know, that's a long time and many contemporary couples may have a difficult time wrapping their heads around our wonderful journey. Two children and three grandchildren have evolved from that love. For all those years, you have been so easy to love, that any man you choose into your heart would only want to cling to your goodness, your unchanging, timeless beauty; and your bravery.

You have battled cancer three times. As I write this, you may be facing a fourth. You have not been alone. Our deep, very deep love for each other has been the emotional chemotherapy that refuses to allow this devoted pairing to end. Your courage is greater than mine. Each one of your strengths enhances my love for you. Your determined will, to keep us together on this earth, is indeed, fierce. You have given my life a higher meaning.

I could not ask any more from you than what you have given. Your unconditional love is felt every day. I know I reciprocate, but as expressed earlier, it is so easy to love you. You make our love uncomplicated; you meet my deep desires and needs and I meet yours. Simple formula. Should we share it with others? I guess I'm doing that by my public Valentine Love Letter to you.

I love you, Charlene. Thanks for our children. Thank you for helping me grow up from that self-centered college student. Thank you for choosing me.

CANCER ... YOU LOSE!

Date: Jan. 2012
Category: Nonfiction
Author: Jeanette Clark Poole
The Prompt: The World Is Divided Into Two Kinds
of People

There are two kinds of people in this world:
The Positives and the Negatives. Those who
aspire to be the very best they can be, and those
who give up without even trying.

Contrary to what our forefathers wrote, I don't
believe: 'All Men are Created Equal'. Because, as I
see it, some people are born with that so-called
'Silver Spoon'. But no matter what our station in
life, or what our circumstances are, we should
strive to do the very best we can. My Mother
always told me, when I was growing up, "Do the
very best you can with what you have." Oprah
Winfrey puts it another way, "Live Your best Life!"

Can anyone even imagine a plight worse than
Hellen Keller's? At 19 months old, she was
stricken with an illness that left her not only blind,
but also deaf and yet, she overcame. I don't see
how on earth she learned to communicate. Yes,
I've seen the movie, 'The Miracle Worker', but I
still can't comprehend. Helen Keller must have
been super intelligent, because she not only
learned to communicate, she actually learned to
speak, and lectured all over the world. She
graduated from Radcliffe College with a Batchelor
of Arts degree at 24 years old. She was the author
of 12 books. In 2003, her birth state of Alabama,

honored her posthumously, by putting her image on their state quarter.

It has been said, that in a "Perfect World" everyone would be born "Rich and Beautiful." However, 'beauty is in the eyes of the beholder.' And, just how much money is Rich? For someone living in the Appalachian Mountains, ten thousand dollars might seem like a fortune. But, most of us would argue, that in today's world, "Someone, with a million dollars isn't really rich". They say that most Million Dollar Lottery Winners are broke within one to two years.

I once knew a young lady who received a million-dollar 'settlement' of some kind, and the first thing she did was to take 'all her friends on an extended trip to New York City (and with that kind of money, one has many friends, some of them brand new friends). That little lady's money lasted less than a year. Now, it's easy to say, "I wouldn't be that foolish," but is it fair to judge other's when we haven't walked in their shoes? Just think how nice it must be to suddenly realize, Hey, I always wanted a Ferrari, or a Jaguar, and now I can actually buy one or both and pay cash!

Some people 'Live in the moment' while others 'Save for a Rainy Day.' My daughter, Marla, was in the former group. She made good money, but spent it as fast as she got it. She collected art, and expensive antiques. She was generous and gave to charities. She loved to travel, and visited all over the United States. She went to the

Bahamas, to Hawaii, and to her favorite country in Europe which was Italy. I often admonished her for not saving for that proverbial rainy day. Although she had a retirement fund, and I believe that her generation will probably be able to collect Social Security, she had no other investments, and didn't own her own home. But, she was happy!

Then, Marla died suddenly, without any warning, of a brain hemorrhage. Only then did I realize, what is positive for one person, is not necessarily positive for another. I truly believe that for Marla 'living in the moment' was the right thing to do and I would have such a huge guilt-trip now if she had listened to me and saved all that money for someone else to be spending now.

And then, there are the Givers and the Takers. It's been said that the Takers may eat better, but the Givers sleep better. Which one are you?

I like what Earl Wilson is credited with saying: He said, "There are three kinds of people in this world–The Haves, the Have-Nots, and those who Have Not Paid For What They Have!

HOW TO ORDER COPIES OF THIS BOOK

To order, simply fill in this Order Form and include your check or credit card authorization. Make check payable to Cypress Cove Publishing.

Mail to:
Cypress Cove Publishing
ATTN: Order Dept.
PO Box 91195
Lafayette, LA 70509-1195

THIS BOOK MAKES A GREAT GIFT!
Do you know any aspiring writers, or those who simply enjoy reading?
Or perhaps you would like to donate copies to a school or library.

( ) **YES, this is a gift:** If you are buying for someone beside yourself, or in addition to yourself, please check the box and write the name and address of the recipients on a separate sheet of paper. We will ship the books to them on your behalf!

Please RUSH me _____ copies of **WGA Anthology 2012-2014** at $14.95 per book, plus a flat fee of $5 shipping & handling no matter how many copies you want. Louisiana residents please add $1.00 sales tax per book.

( ) Enclosed is my check or money order for $_____

( ) **I'd rather charge it.** Please charge $_____ to my ( ) Visa ( ) MC
( ) Discover

Account # _____
Exp. Date_____ CVN code# _____

Cardholder signature: _____
~~~~~~~~~~~~~~~~~~~~~~~~~~~~~~~~~~~
Ordered by:
Name _____
Address_____
City, State, Zip _____
Phone_____ Email_____

QUESTIONS? Phone the Publisher at (888) 606-3257